**Books should be returned on or before the
last date stamped below**

Little Wolf
and the Giant

Sue Porter

SIMON & SCHUSTER

LONDON • SYDNEY • NEW YORK • TOKYO • SINGAPORE • TORONTO

FOR BEST FRIENDS — Danny Carla James David Kirsty Tom Megan David

First published in Great Britain in 1989
by Simon & Schuster Limited

This edition first published in 1991
by Simon & Schuster Young Books
Simon & Schuster Limited
Wolsey House, Wolsey Road
Hemel Hempstead HP2 4SS

Copyright © 1989 Sue Porter

British Library Cataloguing in Publication Data
Porter, Sue
    Little Wolf and the Giant
    I. Title
    823.'914 [J]

ISBN 0-671-69994-6
ISBN 0-7500-0777-X pbk

As Little Wolf was getting ready to visit his Granny, he felt worried. She lived on the other side of a big, spooky wood.
"Are there any giants in the wood?" he asked his Mum.
"Of course not, silly," she said.

Little Wolf set off. But he had only gone a short way, when he heard a dreadful noise.

slurp, slurp, slurp.

"I know there aren't any giants," he said aloud. But, just in case, he speeded up and trotted along at a much quicker pace. Suddenly, he saw a great big rock blocking the path. He didn't slow down at all, but sailed right over the top.

CRASH!

"*Aaargh!*" cried the Giant, who
didn't notice the rock until
he tripped over it.

Little Wolf heard the crash. He didn't
dare to look. He began to shake and started
to run. Suddenly, he saw a great big hole
right in his path. He didn't slow down
at all, but sailed right over the top.

CRASH!

"Aaargh!" cried the Giant, who didn't notice
the hole until he fell right into it.

"Oh no!" shrieked Little Wolf as he heard the crash. "It *is* a giant!" He forced his legs to run faster. Suddenly, he saw a rickety, old bridge ahead. He didn't slow down at all, but sailed right over the top.

SPLASH!

"Aaargh!" cried the Giant as the rickety, old bridge broke under his weight.

"Help! Help!" screamed Little Wolf as he heard the splash close behind him. He looked over his shoulder instead of where he was going and didn't see the fallen tree blocking the path…

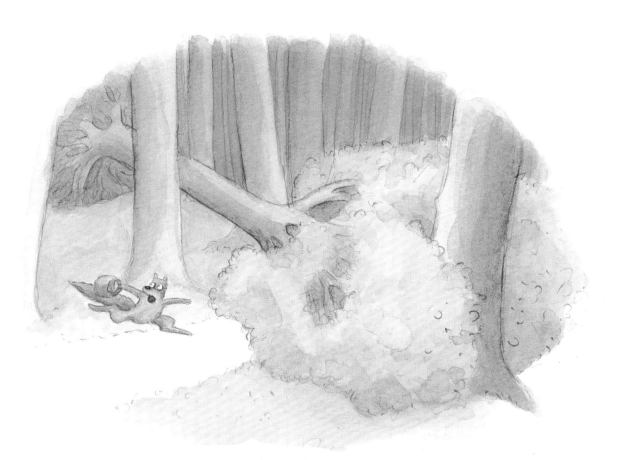

CRASH!

"*Aaargh!*" cried Little Wolf as he tripped and tumbled into the branches. Although he struggled he was tightly trapped. Then, he heard the Giant's footsteps coming closer and closer…

"Save me, save me!" cried Little Wolf. But it was too late. A huge pair of hands grabbed him.
"At last," boomed the big voice of the Giant.

"I've been trying to catch up with you," explained the Giant. "You dropped this cake right at the edge of the wood." "Th-thank you," said Little Wolf, who was still a bit scared. "I thought you were after me."

"Everyone always thinks that," said the Giant, sadly. "I don't have any friends, I look so scary."

"I'll be your friend," replied Little Wolf. "Come and have tea at Granny's with me."

"Yes *please*," said the Giant.

"I'm so glad you're not scared of giants any more."

"But I am scared of witches," said Little Wolf.

"Do you think there are any witches in the wood?"

"Of course not, silly," said the Giant.
And off they set.